SUICIDE GIRLS in the AFTERLIFE

Gina Ranalli

Published by Bloo Skize
Seattle, Washington

Originally published by Afterbirth Books, 2006.

Suicide Girls in the Afterlife
ISBN: 0692393145
ISBN-13: 978-0692393147

Also by Gina Ranalli

Unearthed

Dark Surge

Rumors of My Death

Chemical Gardens

Mother Puncher

Wall of Kiss

Sky Tongues

House of Fallen Trees

Praise the Dead

Ghost Chant

SUICIDE GIRLS
in the
AFTERLIFE

CHAPTER 1

Tramping through the electric forest on a rainy night is suicide.

All around me, tin-foil trees glow silver-white, lightning branches scratching the belly of the black sky which thunder-purrs its pleasure and promises a newborn baby downpour.

Still, the night birds are unfazed by the threatening weather. Back and forth, they sing static to each other and occasionally I get a glimpse of their comet eyes gazing down at me as I pass.

I'm searching for the river of ice, watching where I step and composing a note in my head all at the same time. The note will never be written but I compose it just the same. It makes me feel better to be thinking as I try to avoid stepping on or tripping over any above-ground tree roots. That would be a careless, unappetizing way to die. And embarrassing. Then I'd be remembered not only as a failure at life, but a klutz too.

Hence I walk carefully in the direction I know the river to be. It's the distance that I'm unsure of. Day or night, this forest all looks the same, but at least it's well lit. Sometimes blindingly bright, in fact, especially on a night like this. Everything is alive with anticipation: dead leaves on the ground crackle and pop, rocks buzz softly, flickering white veins across their surfaces, while two blue squirrels chase each other across my path and up a Sagewood tree, chattering drunken nonsense, trailing sparks.

I increase my pace, knowing that the instant rain begins to fall, I'm fried. The entire forest will connect to itself and become a web of electricity, impossible to move through without catching more than a friendly volt.

Tuning out the cacophony of the woods and listening beneath it, I at last hear the clunk clunk clunk of the river. Almost there.

And then I hear the hiss of the first few droplets.

Sprinting towards the river, dodging trees and leaping brush, I wonder if I'll make it. Already, I can feel my hair coming alive, sizzling on my head and reaching for the sky. Moving too fast to avoid a low branch, my shoulder grazes it and I yelp as a jolt shoots all the way down my arm to my fingertips.

Fuck.

I get zapped yet again by misjudging the width between two boulders but I can see the river now, shining like diamonds a mere ten yards away.

Filled with hope at the sight, I dash forward, eyes frantically scanning the trees that live at the very lip of the river, seeking a low enough branch…a long enough branch.

The forest hums louder, grows brighter, as the rain makes contact with its spitting hide and I am sure to die.

But then there is a Brain tree, some of its skeletal roots dancing blurs above the river and I am airborne, grasping the longest vine and flying out over the ice just as the forest goes super-nova and I burn blind.

CHAPTER 2

"Upsy daisy."

I ignore the male voice, comfortable in my slumber.

"Ms. Pogue Eldridge," the voice announces loudly. "Your immediate presence at the Sterling Hotel is humbly requested."

Annoyed, I try to roll over but for some reason find myself paralyzed. To make matters worse, someone—the owner of the voice, I presume—starts tugging my left arm in a further attempt to get me up.

Opening my eyes, I intend to snarl at the stranger, but when I see where I am, all words are momentarily lost to me: in the river, up to my waist in thousands of square ice cubes.

It's daylight now and all around me the forest still sputters here and there, happy in its afterglow. The tentacle branch that I grabbed lies nearby, severed from the Brain tree, though the tree itself is no longer at the river's edge. The ice has carried me downstream a ways, though not far, given its lazy glacial pace.

"We need to get you out of there," says the man

gripping my arm. He's an older guy—sixties perhaps—handsome and dressed in an immaculate white suit that matches his hair and trimmed beard exactly. "Have to get you checked in."

"Am I dead?" I ask.

"You're dead weight, I can tell you that." He continues pulling at me.

"I don't feel cold. I'm dead right?"

He pauses in his struggle. "What do you think?"

I shrug. "I hope so. I tried to kill myself last night."

He straightens up, crosses his arms and clucks disapprovingly. "Suicides are a classless bunch. Now, get yourself out of that ice. We don't have all day."

Without thinking about it, I obey him, climbing out of the river and standing on top of it, facing him. I notice his eyes are the same shade of blue as the playful squirrels I saw the night before.

"That's better," he says. "Now, allow me to introduce myself. My name is Salvadore. I will be your escort to the Sterling Hotel and I suggest we get a move on. You have a reservation."

"I do?"

"You do." He offers me his arm. "Shall we?"

CHAPTER 3

Salvadore leads me through the electric forest until I'm completely disoriented. East, west? I don't know, and Salvadore isn't saying. For a while, I assume we're lost, but he assures me that he knows exactly where we're headed. The Sterling Hotel, of course. Wherever that is.

I still have no clue where we are when we finally make our way out, but it's nowhere I recognize. A hot dusty road, dry despite last night's rain, quiet but for the sound of chirping insects. Huge cliffs on either side, lined with enormously tall, purple-leafed Sagewoods. Up ahead, a stone tunnel, its throat yawning and cavity-black.

"Are we going in there?"

"It's the only way there is," Salvadore says matter-of-factly.

"Well, are there any sidewalks? There's none out here. What if a car comes?"

"No car will come."

I frown. "How do you know?"

"Look." He jerks a thumb behind us and, confused, I turn and immediately see what he means by 'the only way there is.'

There's nothing there.

No road, no cliffs, no trees.

Nothing.

Behind us lays a vast white emptiness, a new canvas without borders. No left, no right. No up, no down. Just white nothing, snug up to our backs.

My heart stammers. "What the hell…what's going on?"

Indifferent, Salvadore reaches into an inner pocket of his pristine white jacket and pulls out a small roll of candy. He pops one into his mouth and offers me the roll. "Life Saver?"

I stare at him.

He shakes the candy. "It's green," he says temptingly. "Fungus flavor."

"Salvadore, where did the road go?"

Deciding he'd like the green candy for himself, he deftly flips it from the roll and into his mouth before returning the Life Savers to his pocket.

"Salvadore?"

"Now is all there is," he tells me with a small smile. "It's best not to give it much thought. Just come along. We need to get you checked in."

We resume our journey but I've only gone five or six steps when I sneak a glance back and see the white again. Fascinated, I turn around and retrace my steps, peering into the nothing for some sense of…something. There's a moment when I think I see movement in there, in the nothing, and I stop, straining my eyes. And then I see it again, a flickering flash, white on purest white and I reach out my hand, wanting to touch the motion despite a sudden and distinct chill that surrounds me.

"No!" Salvadore has come up beside me once more,

swatting my hand away. "You don't want to do that, Pogue."

"Why not? What's in there?"

He opens his mouth as if to speak, then closes it again. "Come on. We need to—"

"Get me checked in, I know, but…" I look at the wall of white and then back at him. "You're not going to tell me?"

"There's nothing to tell. Now, come. Look, we're almost there."

Reluctantly, I face forward and see the tunnel. "We're not that close."

"We'll be there in five minutes if you can manage to keep your feet moving."

The impatience in his voice tells me that I'll be better off just doing as I'm told for the time being and the thought distresses me. Dead and still taking orders? What a drag…

CHAPTER 4

Salvadore speaks the truth. As we walk forward, the tunnel's opening grows nearer much faster than it should have. It seems as if it too is moving, closing the distance between us, meeting us halfway.

But, of course, the tunnel can't be moving. That's impossible.

Nonetheless, we arrive at the mouth within five minutes, though it had previously appeared to be at least a half-hour walk. I stop in my tracks and peer uneasily into the darkness of that black, gaping cavern.

Beside me, Salvadore stops as well. Apparently sensing my trepidation, he says, "There's nothing to fear, I can assure you."

I glance at him skeptically before assessing everything around me once more. Before me, a tunnel of darkness. To either side, what appears to be dense forest and behind me, nothing. I look down and wonder if the road beneath my feet is anything more than a mere illusion.

"How do I know this isn't a tunnel to hell?" I ask.

"There's only one way to find out," he says. "Besides,

what choice do you have? You can either enter and see where it leads or you can stand here on the brink for all eternity."

I consider the options, and decide that maybe staying right where I am forever wouldn't be such a bad thing. I'd have the trees, the distant sound of birds and insects. Quite relaxing, actually.

Once again reading my thoughts, Salvadore says, "You'd stand here for about an hour before boredom and anxiety set in and then you'd steel yourself and enter the tunnel anyway. But, you'd be doing it alone, since I have other appointments to make and don't have time to hang around and baby you."

I'm tempted to argue—certainly it would take more than an hour for me to get bored—but I know he's right. Eventually, I'd start to get freaked out, sandwiched between vast white and black, and would probably end up lunging into one or the other without any sense of what I was doing.

Clenching my fists, I inhale deeply and take the first steps into the black tunnel, Salvadore at my side.

CHAPTER 5

I have no idea how long we're in the tunnel but it seems to be only an instant. In that instant however, I lose all sense of self: there is no up or down, I can't hear, see or smell anything. I can't feel my body or the ground beneath my feet. I have no sense of any movement whatsoever, much less feel myself walking. If Salvadore is still beside me, his presence is undetectable.

And in a blink of an eye, we emerge on the other side, whole and still side by side, standing atop a high green hill and looking down upon a brilliant and sparkling glass city.

Instinct tells me that if I turn to glance back at the tunnel it will no longer exist, but I look anyway and see that I'm right. Only lush forest lies behind us now, cool and dark, inviting in its impossibility.

I face front again, gaze down at the bright buildings, sunlight glinting off windows and chrome, and release the breath I have pent up in my lungs, the very same breath I had taken just before entering the tunnel.

"Welcome to the Virgin City, Pogue," Salvadore says. "Spectacular, isn't it?"

Nodding, it takes a moment for the name of the place to register with me. When it does, I look at him. "Did you say Virgin City?"

"I did. You've heard of it?" He seems surprised.

"No…but why virgin? Is that one of the prerequisites for getting into heaven? Because if it is, you definitely brought me to the wrong place. I haven't been a—"

He hushes me by holding up his hand and shaking his head. "It's nothing like that. Look."

My eyes follow his pointing finger to the sky, to the sun, which it turns out, isn't a sun at all but the gentle smiling face of the Virgin Mary. She is gazing down at us with a pleased expression beneath her baby-blue cloak, nodding her approval and giving me a wink.

Salvadore raises a hand and waves to her, nudging me to do the same. I do and her grin becomes wider, all teeth, white and blinding.

I look away, blotches of light dancing on my retinas. "Damn," I say. "She sure is bright."

"She's happy to see you," Salvadore says.

Rubbing my eyes in an attempt to see again, I say, "What's up with this anyway? I'm not even Catholic."

Ignoring my question, Salvadore places a hand on my elbow and says, "Come on. We have a bus to catch."

"A bus?"

CHAPTER 6

Sure enough, after we descend the hill and enter the city, we walk down an impossibly clean street to the corner, where there is a bus stop and a bench. Salvadore sits down and pulls a hanky out of an inner jacket pocket and blows his nose.

"Where is everyone?" I ask. I can't help but notice that we are the only people within sight. And not only are we alone on the street, but neither is there any traffic. Absolutely nothing moves anywhere, except us. Not even a single candy wrapper blows by. "This is kinda creepy," I say.

"Maybe they all have the day off," Salvadore says, returning the hanky to its pocket. I start to reply but the appearance of an immaculate city bus distracts me. It appears to be brand new, sparkling clean, like the buildings themselves.

"Here we are," Salvadore says, rising from the bench. "That wasn't too long of a wait."

The bus door hisses open and Salvadore gestures for me to board first. I climb the steps cautiously, eyeing the black female driver with more than a little suspicion. She smiles cheerfully at me as I look around for a coin box that isn't there.

"No toll," Salvadore says from behind me. "Just take a seat."

I do as I'm told, choosing the first bench on the left, and slide over to the window. Salvadore sits beside me as the door closes and the bus pulls out onto the deserted street.

"Almost there now," he says.

Frowning, I look from him to the view outside the window just as the bus is pulling over at what must be the next bus stop. Before I can make any reaction whatsoever, he has risen from the seat and is exiting the bus again. I leap up, hurrying after him.

Once more on the sidewalk, I say, "Was that even half a block? We could have just walked."

Salvadore isn't listening though. Instead, he is smiling up at the building before us. As I turn to follow his gaze with my own, I notice that it is no longer day but night here in the Virgin City. A comfortable, breezy night, late summer or early fall by the feel of it.

And we are no longer alone either. People are everywhere; happy people, every last one of them. Milling around, talking, laughing, smoking, joking. Some of them are dressed to the nines while others appear to be homeless and in rags. A good number of them I hear commenting on the beautiful evening, the stars and the moon.

Glancing skyward, I once again see the Mother Mary smiling, replacing the moon as she had replaced the sun. Her countenance is more than just the moon though. Peering closing at the stars, I can just make out her blue cloak on each and every one of them. A billion Marys hang above us, twinkling and joyful and I have to look away quickly, suddenly feeling a bit queasy.

"Overwhelmed?" Salvadore asks, placing a hand on my shoulder. Without waiting for my response, he continues and gestures at the building before us, "Why don't we go inside."

For the first time, I focus my attention on the grand white structure lit up as if for a debutante's ball. "What is this place?"

"This," Salvadore says, "is the Sterling Hotel."

CHAPTER 7

We move through the crowd and begin ascending the hotel's two dozen marble stairs to the revolving glass doors that allow us access into the elegant building and its beautifully refined lobby.

Despite all the bustling outside, the lobby is relatively calm. A few people are seated on lush white furniture, speaking in soothing tones and smiling and nodding at each other.

"This is too weird for me," I say, stopping in my tracks. "Why does everyone seem so nice?"

Salvadore shrugs. "They're mostly pretty nice, I suppose."

"Is this the afterlife? A fancy hotel? Because if it is, I have to tell you, I'm kind of disappointed."

He stares at me, looking vaguely annoyed. "We have to get you checked in. As I think I mentioned, I have other appointments."

"Are most people happy to find out this is the afterlife?" I glance around again. "I can't believe they're happy about it."

Salvadore sighs. "This isn't quite the afterlife, Pogue."

"It's not?"

"I'm not supposed to say anything about this. But, frankly, you're getting on my nerves. You were supposed to go to the seminar."

"What seminar?"

"The seminar that would explain all this to you." He gestures at our surroundings. "This is just where we have to put you up for a while. Free of charge, of course."

"Put me up? What are you talking about?" I am beginning to suspect that I'm not actually dead at all. My suicide attempt must have failed and now I'm in some loony-bin, probably imagining all of this. Salvadore is probably a head shrinker. Unless I'm imagining him too. "I'm not really dead, am I? Fuck! I knew I'd manage to screw it up somehow." I stand there shaking my head, disgusted with myself.

"You're dead all right," Salvadore says.

I look at him, skeptical. "You're just saying that to make me feel better."

He holds up a hand, his thumb and pinky folded down. "Scout's Honor, Pogue. You are indeed dead."

It takes me a second to decide whether or not I believe him, but then I smile. He does seem like an honest old coot. "Oh, thank God. I was sick of my life. You have no idea."

Rolling his eyes, he says, "Can we get back to business, please?"

"Oh, right. Sure. You were saying something about a seminar?"

"Yes. But never mind that because you won't need to attend it now."

"Why not?" For some reason I feel slightly jilted.

Salvadore is starting to look extremely distressed and

impatient, so I just forget my last question and resign myself to let him tell me whatever it is he needs to tell me. Which turns out to be this: "Both Heaven and Hell are undergoing some renovations right now. Everyone who's already there is fine. But we have nowhere to put up all the newcomers, like yourself. You have to understand, both places—but particularly Hell—are growing in scope and size every day. So, every few millennia, we have to make renovations here and there. Spruce the place up, if you will."

I listen to all this, nodding as if I know what he's talking about. When it seems like he's finished, I say, "So, you put everyone in a hotel?"

"That's correct, yes."

It's my turn to sigh and I let out a huge one. "Wow. That's pretty fucked up. When will the renovations be complete?"

He smiles, like he's finally on familiar ground again. "Any day now." He holds out a hand to me. "Shall we get you checked in now?"

I think about it, regarding his outstretched hand carefully. "I guess so," I say finally, taking his hand and allowing him to lead me to the front desk where a clerk with a pencil-thin mustache awaits, smiling happily like he has the best job in the world.

"Check in," Salvadore says. "Eldridge, Pogue."

The clerk nods and types something into his computer. "Ah, yes. Suicide. Electrocution was it?"Frowning, I say, "What does that have to do with anything?"

Pencil-mustache's smile widens. "Only everything," he says.

"Electrocution," Salvadore confirms and Mustache bends down, rummages beneath the counter for a minute and comes up with a keycard. "You'll be on the fifth floor. Room 658."

I take the card and look at it. One side has the picture of a hippie guy, grinning and giving the peace sign. I flip it over and the other side shows a pouty Goth, wearing black eyeliner and looking sullen. "Who are these guys?" I ask.

"Well," Salvadore says. "My job here is done. Good luck to you, Pogue." He holds out his hand to be shaken.

"You're just gonna leave me here?" I say. "I thought you were my escort."

"I was. And I escorted you. Now, if you'll excuse me—"

"You should at least escort me to my room," I interrupt. "That would be the gentlemanly thing to do."

"Actually, Pogue," he says, "truth be told, I wasn't even supposed to be your escort. I was just filling in for someone else."

I fold my arms across my chest. "Who?"

Turning around to face the doors, Salvadore points and says, "Her."

I look and see a big black woman just spinning out of the revolving door. Once inside, she turns to the person behind her, just entering. "Get your scrawny white ass in here, bitch," the black woman bellows. "Do I look like I got all day?"

The person she's yelling at—a teenage girl—looks pissed. She's dressed like a street kid, in ratty clothes that are too big for her and her hair hangs to her shoulders in long greasy strips.

The black woman, dressed in a big purple dress with swirls of green and orange all over it, grabs the teenager by the arm and starts pulling her over to the check-in counter.

"This is Katina," the woman tells Mr. Mustache. "Another damn fool who went and offed herself before she's even old enough to vote."

"I told you," Katina says, trying to pull free of the woman's grasp, "I didn't off myself. At least not on purpose."

The black woman releases the girl and puts her hands on her hips. "Uh huh. Did you or did you not stick a needle in your arm?"

Katina looks at the floor and says nothing.

"Uh huh," the woman continues. "And did that needle contain enough smack to drop an elephant or did it not?"

Again, Katina makes no reply.

"Uh huh," the woman repeats, turning back to the desk. "Suicide."

"It was an accident!" Katina cries.

Beside me Salvadore shakes his head sadly while watching this exchange.

"Honey," the woman says to Katina. "There are no accidents. Almost every-damn-body is a suicide when you get right down to it. Those are just the rules. You smoke and die of lung cancer? The big boy upstairs says suicide. You eat at McDonald's every damn day of your life and your heart turns into a little ball of cement? Suicide. You get drunk and drive into a tree or turn your liver into jelly? Suicide. Don't matter how long or short it takes people. Fact is, most people kill themselves and it's no use arguing about it. Like I said, those are the rules."

Katina looks at me, her eyes pleading.

I shrug. "I did it on purpose. Sorry."

Salvadore clears his throat and addresses the big black woman. "Ms. Stardust, I'd like to introduce you to Pogue. She was supposed to be your pick-up."

"Is that so?" The woman gives me the once over.

"Well, sorry I missed you, sweetheart, but as you can tell I've had my hands full."

It's only when I'm looking at her face to face that I notice the Adam's apple bobbing up and down in her throat. And now that I'm thinking about it, her voice is an octave or so too low.

The fact that she's really a dude is only of passing interest to me. "Nice to meet you…uh…Ms. Stardust."

"This sucks," Katina blurts abruptly. "It's not fair! I have to go to hell for killing myself, even though I didn't really kill myself?"

"I don't make the rules, sweetheart," Ms Stardust says, examining her long red fingernails. "I just follow 'em."

"Hell?" I say, alarmed. I look at Salvadore. "What is she talking about hell for?"

He looks down at his watch. "Would you look at the time? I can't believe how far behind I'm running!" And before I can stop him, he walks briskly through the lobby and out through the revolving doors.

I stare after him, my jaw hanging. "That son of a bitch."

Ms. Stardust barks a laugh. "Honey, you're lucky he took time out of his busy schedule to escort you over here. He almost never lowers himself for the suicides."

"What do you mean?"

"Oh, that Salvadore. He usually does the rich white people who died old. Or sometimes young ones, if they were in tip-top condition and had nothing to do with their own deaths, which according to the rules, amounts to pretty much the same thing."

"I'm not following you," I say.

"Look," Ms. Stardust says, addressing both Katina and I. "Pretty much everyone is considered a suicide. The only ones who aren't, are the ones who could afford to take care of themselves, you see what I'm saying? Rich folks that could go to their fancy-ass gyms, buy the best organic foods, get the best medical care. Those are the folks that are in the luxury suites right this very minute and those are the folks old Sally escorts over here. You were just a fluke, honey."

I try to absorb what she's saying and can't quite make it work in my head.

Katina says, "So, in other words, the rich people own fucking heaven too? What the fuck is up with that? That's not right!"

Ms. Stardust says, "Umm hmm. Death is no fairer than life, sweetheart. Don't let anybody tell you different." The she turns to Mustache Man and starts getting Katina checked in while Katina and I eye each other with morbid curiosity.

"You really offed yourself then, huh?"

I nod. "But I had my reasons."

"No reason is a good enough reason," Ms. Stardust says over her shoulder.

Katina reaches into the pocket of her gray hoodie and pulls out a pack of gum. Juicy Fruit. Thoughtfully, she unwraps a piece and then offers me the pack. I accept and by the time Ms. Stardust has returned her attention to us, we are both merrily chewing away and not talking.

Ms. Stardust hands Katina her keycard. "You're on the sixth floor. Room 544."

I pause in my chewing. "I'm on the fifth floor."

Arching an eyebrow at me, Ms. Stardust says, "Is that right? Honey, I'm surprised you're not on the first or second."

"Because I killed myself on purpose?"

"That's right."

"And Katina here killed herself by accident, so she

gets to be on a higher floor."

"Now you're catching on. And you know what? I'd love to stay here and chit-chat with you lovely girls all night long, but my shift isn't over yet and I got more junkies to claim."

Still chewing her gum, Katina asks, "Are you a grim reaper or what?"

Ms. Stardust puts her hands on her hips and looks down at Katina, her face scrunched into a frown. "Now, why would you want to go insult me like that? Do I look like a grim reaper to you?"

"Well, no, but…how should we know what a grim reaper looks like? It's not like I've ever been dead before."

"Umm hmm," Ms. Stardust says, still looking perturbed. "Anyway, you ladies enjoy your stay here at the Sterling Hotel. If you need anything, just dial zero on your room phones and Louis over there will see that you get it. Okay, then? Good. Bye-bye."

Katina and I watch Ms. Stardust sashay across the lobby and out into the night, both of us chewing our gum much louder than we have to, as if the normal act of chewing gum will rub off on this extremely strange situation.

Once she's gone, we look at each other and shrug.

"Guess I'll go find my room," I say.

"Yeah, me too."

Together we make our way over to the elevators, Katina snapping her gum every few seconds. I push the up button and the door immediately opens. Inside, a young pale guy stands there, just watching us.

I say, "Are you like, the elevator guy?"

"The elevator guy? No, I'm Ago."

"Pardon me?" By now Katina and I have entered the

elevator and the shiny silver door has slid shut.

"That's my name," the guy says. "Ago."

"Ah."

"That's a pretty stupid name, you ask me," Katina says.

Ago gives her a wounded look, so I quickly say, "Don't mind her. She's pissed because they're saying she's a suicide."

"Pretty much everyone is a suicide," Ago says.

"Not me!" Katina snaps her gum angrily and pushes the button for the sixth floor. "Hey," she says. "There's a button here that says 4 ½."

"That's my floor," Ago says. "You don't want to go there."

"Why not?" Katina asks.

"Because it doesn't really exist."

Katina and I both look at Ago as if he's slipped a groove. Finally, I say, "I don't know. Now you have me curious."

"Me too," says Katina. "I'm getting off on your floor."

Ago sighs. "I knew I shouldn't have told you."

The elevator stops at every floor but no other passengers get on. From what we can see, the hotel looks like a pretty shabby one.

We arrive and leave the fourth floor without incident and then the elevator lurches violently, causing all three of us to lose our balance. Katina and I fall down, but Ago is holding onto the rail, obviously expecting it.

"You could have warned us," I say, getting to my feet.

"No, shit," Katina agrees, standing up. "I swallowed my gum."

Ago ignores us and begins trying to pry open the elevator doors with his fingers. He grunts and groans with the effort, occasionally swearing under his breath. "Can one of you give me a hand?"

"Sure." I go over and start to yank on the doors. A minute later, it budges and we can clearly see that we're stuck between floors. Forcing the doors wide enough for a person to be able to squeeze through takes another few seconds and then I stand back to admire our handy work. "Looks like we'll have to climb up."

"Always do," Ago says and begins to do exactly that.

Outside the elevator, there is nothing to be seen. Just darkness.

"Is the power out on your floor?" I ask.

"There's never any power on 4 ½," Ago says, hauling himself up and clambering into the darkness. Then he disappears out of sight, as if the darkness has swallowed him whole.

"Ago?" I call. "Where did you go, Ago?"

As if from very far away, his voice drifts down to us. "Just be on your way. This is no place for you."

Of course this does nothing but make me want to check out floor 4 ½ all the more. "Give me a boost," I say to Katina.

For a second she looks like she may protest, then she shrugs and makes a step out of her laced hands.

Using my elbows for leverage, I pull myself up and exit the elevator into nothing but thick blackness. I turn around to see the inside of the elevator, though it is no longer directly behind me. It's a long ways off, a skinny rectangle of light that seems to be receding even as I watch. "What the hell…"

"You made a mistake," Ago says, his voice beside my ear now.

"How can you stay on this floor? You should definitely ask to be moved someplace else."

Ago chuckles. "I wish. But this is Purgatory."

"Purga—wait. What?"

And it's as if the word being spoken aloud has triggered some kind of limbo switch, because my body flattens and stretches and twists in a way that the human body is definitely not meant to do. Or maybe it's the darkness that is actually changing shape, but if that's the case then that would mean that I have become part of the darkness and the thought—in addition to the ceaseless shape-shifting—suddenly makes me feel like vomiting, which I almost certainly would have done if I'd been able to determine where my stomach was or if it was even still part of my body.

"Are you guys okay?" Katina. From very far away. "Guys?"

I try to respond that I'm most definitely not okay but I have no words. I'm not even sure if I have a mouth or vocal cords. I decide that if I ever get out of here, the hotel management is going to get an earful. They'll wish they'd never even heard the name Pogue Eldritch. Maybe they'll even realize that this whole Purgatory thing was a bad idea. A very bad idea.

I'm just starting to compose a letter of complaint in my mind when I feel something like a boot plant itself firmly in what I suspect is my ass, but I can't really be sure. It's more of a mental push than a physical one and the next thing I know I'm falling down into light.

I crash with a grunt and look up to see Katina looking down at me. "How was it?" she asks, snapping a new piece of gum, her expression bored.

For the second time, I pick myself up off the elevator floor and say, "I don't want to talk about it."

Katina gives me a snotty look and says, "Whatev. Help me get this stupid door closed."

CHAPTER 8

Together we manage to close the elevator door and then we're rising again, but only for a few seconds. Then the door whooshes open and we're looking out into what appears to be an average hotel hallway.

"Fifth floor," Katina says, watching me expectantly.

"I see that! Don't you think I see that?"

Katina waves towards the hall. "Well, fucking go."

I clear my throat. Take a deep breath. Gingerly stick my foot outside the elevator and test the floor of the hallway. Seems solid, so I step out and then turn back just as the elevator door is sliding closed. I raise my hand to wave goodbye to Katina but then she reaches out, stopping the door from closing. "Fuck this," she says, getting off the elevator to stand beside me. "I don't want to do this shit alone."

Who can blame her? She's just a kid after all.

I pull my keycard out of my pocket and say, "Room 735. That's funny. I could have sworn it was a different number before."

"Isn't 735 kind of high too?" Katina asks. "This place

doesn't seem big enough to have that many rooms."

We consider this for a moment and then shrug in unison. "Oh, well," I say, looking up and down the hall. The nearest room is numbered 737. "I guess we're pretty much here already."

At 735, I slip the keycard into its slot and a little green light flashes. I open the door cautiously, unsure of what to expect.

When I flip the light switch, however, the room appears to be completely normal. A carbon copy of a million other hotel rooms across the globe.

There is a double bed, a floral pastel bedspread across it, a small desk, a lavender lounge chair, a little table with two straight-backed chairs tucked neatly beneath it. A closet with a wooden sliding door. A night table with a white ceramic lamp and that's it.

"This is so not how I pictured Heaven to be," Katina says.

"It's not Heaven," I remind her. "Heaven is under construction, remember?"

"Whatever," she says, plopping herself down onto the bed. "I can't believe you don't even have a mini-bar."

"Yeah," I say. "That sucks."

I go over to the one window in the room and pull back the pink drapes. Outside, there is a mountain range, gray with snowy peaks. Quite beautiful, except that it's moving. Rolling past the window as if it were the backdrop of a movie. "Shit," I mutter. "The mountains are moving. How messed up is that?"

Katina comes over and looks out. "The mountains aren't moving. We are."

"Really?" I look closer at the mountains. "It doesn't feel like we're moving."

She sighs loudly and moves away from the window.

"Well, we are. The hotel is flying or some shit."

I watch for another minute or two and determine that Katina is correct. Though it can't be felt, the hotel is indeed flying. I wonder where we are. The Rocky Mountains? The Andes? My stomach lurches and I have to turn away from the window.

Katina is sitting at the table, looking at a menu. "Are you hungry?" she asks. "I'm starving."

Sitting down across from her, I ask, "Is there room service?"

"Surprisingly, yes. At least according to this there is, but the menu is kind of…uh…sparse."

"Give me that." I lean over and pluck it from her fingers. Studying the menu, I say "What the hell? 'Floors six and lower (excluding floors one and lower) can choose from a wide variety of our house baked pies, day or night, free of charge.' Pies? That's all we get? I was hoping for nice plate of pasta in white sauce."

"Yeah, and I could go for a big bloody steak but it looks like we're SOL." Katina leans back in her chair and puts her feet on the table. "Did you look at the kinds of pies they have?"

I look down at the menu again. "What's rock pie?"

"Beats me. Probably made with rocks, is my guess."

I get up and go over to the phone on the nightstand. I dial zero and wait for someone to pick up. It takes them several minutes, but when they finally do, I recognize Mustache Man's voice right away. "Hi," I say. "Yeah, this is room…uh…" I look at Katina and snap my fingers, pointing to the keycard on the table. She picks it up and says, "631."

Frowning at her, I repeat the number into the phone. "We're kind of hungry up here and noticed that the menu says we're only allowed to have pies."

"The pies are excellent, I assure you madam," says Mustache Man.

"I'm sure they are, but you know…we're hungry for something a little more substantial than pie right now."

"House rules," he says crisply.

"House rules," I repeat, trying to sound indignant.

Katina jumps out of the chair and barrels over to me, grabbing the phone out of my hand. "Listen, buddy, we think your house rules suck, so why don't you just send us the menu that all the rich people on the upper floors are getting?"

I sit down on the edge of the bed and watch as she listens. It seems like she listens for a long time. Then: "Okay, fine. Whatever. But it better be good." Then she slams the phone down into its cradle. "Fucking wanker," she says to it.

"Are they sending us another menu?" I ask.

"Nope," she replies, heading towards the bathroom. "He said he was sending up pie."

Groaning, I flop back on the bed and look at the ceiling. Oddly, it's covered with tire tread marks of all shapes and sizes. Thin treads that could have been made by a little wagon of some sort, bicycle treads, all the way up to treads that could have only been made by an SUV. I mention it to Katina who lies down beside me and points. "I think that one is from a grocery cart," she says. "I used to work in a grocery store."

"Hmm," I say.

Someone knocks on the door and Katina jumps up to answer it. I don't move. I'm pretty sure I don't want to know who it is, but nevertheless, Katina says, "It's room service with our pie."

"Great," I say sarcastically.

"I'll just put it over here on the table," says a new

female voice.

I sit up to see a strange alien/human hybrid in a tuxedo shirt and black trousers crossing the room and carrying a silver tray with a covered dish, plates, and silverware on it. She smiles at me, big black alien eyes blinking slowly. "Hi. I'm Jane 62," she says with her tiny slit of a mouth. She puts the tray on the table and uncovers the pie. It looks like a regular pie but it sounds like there's music coming from it, very faintly.

"Is there a Jane 63?" Katina asks.

"Not that I know of," Jane 62 replies, cutting into the pie with a huge knife.

I get off the bed and go over to the table, leaning over to listen to the pie. Jane 62 dishes out a slice and suddenly the room is filled with loud opera music, a woman bellowing in what I think is Italian.

"Opera pie," she says, handing me the plate. "It's quite delicious."

Crinkling my nose, I say, "I hate opera." If I could, I'd crinkle my ears as well.

"Guess we should have gotten the rock pie after all," Katina says, taking her plate.

The pie looks like cherry, but I have no intention of eating it. It's giving me a headache and I hand it back to Jane 62. "I'm not hungry right now," I say loudly, to be heard over the music.

Katina decides not to eat it either. "Let's try to get up to a higher floor and find some real food," she suggests.

"Good idea," I say. I turn to Jane 62. "Will you get this out of here? I really can't stand opera."

"We also have a nice country pie," she says pleasantly. "Apple flavored and not quite as loud. Would you like me to bring one up?"

"No!" Katina and I say together.

Jane 62 looks hurt but starts stacking the plates of pie back onto the tray and covering them. Immediately, the volume of the music becomes at least tolerable. "You'll have a hard time getting to the higher floors," Jane 62 says. "It would be much easier to go down than up."

"Why is that?" I ask.

"It's just the rules," she replies.

"Fuck!" Katina blurts. "I'm so sick of hearing about the rules."

"The guests on the upper floors have entitlement issues," Jane 62 explains. "Most of them are not very pleasant."

"Rich people," I say. "Why am I not surprised?"

"I don't care," Katina says. "I just want to get out of this room. I'm bored."

"We could go check out your room," I suggest."

She nods. "Maybe I'll have a better menu."

Jane 62 asks what floor Katina's room is on, then shakes her head. "You can go up there," she says to Katina. "You can't," she says to me.

"That's retarded," I say.

Katina starts bouncing around. "I'm bored! I don't care where we go. Let's just go!"

We follow Jane 62 out into the hall, me patting my pocket to make sure I have my keycard on me.

Outside my door is a cart filled with covered trays and it sounds like a dozen different radio stations playing at once. Jane 62 starts pushing the cart down the hall and the tangled music starts to recede a bit.

"Why don't you come with us?" I ask when she pauses at the room next door to mine.

She turns back. "Upstairs? I'm not allowed up there either."

"Why not?"

"This is my floor," she says. "We're all assigned our floor and we're not supposed to leave it."

"That's bullshit," I tell her. "Why would you let anyone tell you what to do like that? What is this, a prison?"

Jane 62 looks uncertain, the gray-green skin of her forehead wrinkling slightly as though she's worried. "I have always wanted to see other parts of the hotel."

"Hey!" Katina says suddenly. "We should go back to that limbo floor and get that guy too. What was his name again?"

"Ago," I say.

"Yeah, him. What do you think? Party in my room?"

"Sounds good to me." I look at Jane 62. "You only live once. Fuck the rules."

She stays where she is, so I shrug and Katina and I head for the elevator. Just as I'm pushing the button, Jane 62 jogs over and says, "I hope I don't get caught."

"Will you get fired or something?" I ask.

"I have no idea. I don't even get paid."

For some reason this strikes me as funny and I start laughing. Katina cracks up too, but Jane 62 just stands there looking thoughtful.

The elevator opens and the three of us climb in. I push the button for 4 ½ and when we get there, we have to pry open the doors again.

"Ago!" I yell into the darkness. "You in there?"

"Get your ass over here," Katina shouts. "We're having a mutiny!"

I laugh again and together Katina and I scream for Ago and finally he shows himself. He has to crouch down and stick his head into the elevator so we can see him. "What kind of mutiny?" he asks.

"We're gonna explore the hotel," I tell him.

He seems puzzled. "Why?"
"Why not?" I counter.
"Well, we might run into Lucy for one thing."
Jane 62 lets out a little gasp that might be fright.
"Who the fuck is Lucy?" Katina demands.
His face deadly serious, Ago says, "Lucifer."

CHAPTER 9

"Lucifer," I say. "As in, the devil? That Lucifer?"

"The one and only," Ago says. "But, from what I heard, it's best if you don't call him the devil to his face. He's pretty sensitive about it."

I purse my lips, carefully considering this new information.

Beside me, Katina is laughing. "I'm gonna get to meet Satan in the flesh? This is too awesome! I don't even believe in him!"

"You will soon enough," Ago says and climbs down into the elevator. "But, what the hell. Purgatory is getting boring anyway."

Clapping him on the back, I say, "Great. One more person for our revolt."

The elevator doors slide shut and I push the button for the 6th floor. The box gives a lurch, jarring us all, but then doesn't move.

"See?" Jane 62 says. "We're not allowed up there."

"What about me?" Katina protests. "My room is on the 6th floor!"

"You could go up there if we weren't with you," Jane 62 explains. "But since we are, the elevator won't go any higher."

"It's like a built-in security system," Ago adds.

"Well, that's just great," I say sarcastically. "Why didn't you guys tell us this before?"

"We never tried to go up before," Jane 62 says. "We just heard that this would happen and apparently it's true."

"Great," I say again. "Can we go down to the lower floors?"

"Why would you want to go down?" Ago asks, as if it's the most preposterous idea he's ever heard.

I don't bother answering him and just start pushing buttons. The elevator comes back to life, lowering us slowly.

"Oh, shit," Ago whispers, while Jane 62 makes that gasping sound again.

"What's wrong?" Katina asks them. "Scared of a little Beelzebub are you?" She laughs maniacally, pointing and teasing them.

CHAPTER 10

A second later the elevator comes to a stop and the doors open onto a floor that doesn't look very different from mine. A little more rundown, but that's about it. The four of us tromp out and then split up, knocking on doors and trying to get people to join us in our little rebellion. Mostly people just give us weird looks and politely refuse. A couple times we have doors slammed in our faces. A few of the guests won't open their doors at all, but yell curses at us just the same.

We go down to the next floor and find it to be even more raggedy than the previous one. Here the wallpaper is peeling off the walls and the carpets have stains and cigarette burns and the room doors are all dirty. The lights in the ceiling fixtures flicker sporadically and on more than one occasion we find ourselves in almost complete darkness.

Again, we have no luck and pile back into the elevator, both Ago and Jane 62 becoming increasingly nervous.

When the doors open on the next lower floor, we see that it is in even worse condition than the last. The ceiling leaks and the hallway is strewn with trash. There's shouting coming from behind several of the doors, as well as the sound of people weeping. I go to knock on the door of room 256 and the only response I get is something thrown and smashed against the other side of it.

At the far end of the hall, two guys come running out of a room, one chasing the other with a huge meat cleaver and screaming, "I'll chop your fucking head off, you prick!" The first one plows into Katina, almost knocking her over and then barrels down the hallway towards me. I flinch as they race by and then they run into another room, slamming the door behind themselves.

"Maybe this wasn't such a great idea," Katina calls down to me.

I open my mouth to agree, but the door behind me suddenly swings open and I turn to see an older woman standing there in a slinky red robe. She looks somewhat like Marilyn Monroe, if Marilyn had lived to enter her mid-fifties and drank hard liquor every day of her life. She's smoking a cigarette in one of those long cigarette holders and looking at me from beneath eyelids painted a ridiculous shade of blue.

"What's this you're yelling about, honey?" she asks, exhaling smoke through her nostrils.

"Uh…" I hesitate, but then tell her about what we were doing. She listens silently, smoking, without expression.

"Sounds like a real gas," she croaks, when I finish. "I ain't got nothing better to do."

By now, the others have joined me and are regarding this woman with blatant skepticism.

"What's your name?" I ask, out of politeness.

She grins at me, showing off her yellowed crooked

teeth. "The name's Lithia, darlin'. And who might you all be?"

I introduce myself and everyone else.

"Pleased ta meet ya," she greets everyone in turn. Then: "Yep, I reckon I'll come along for the party. I'm sick to death of this hellhole. You're all from above, eh?"

I tell her that Katina and I are, but Jane 62 is sort of an employee of the hotel and Ago is from Purgatory.

Lithia nods. "Gotta be better than this shit. You see where they put me? Only a floor or two above Hell, that's where. Those fucking bastards. I was a Rockette once upon a time and this is how they treat me! Look at these yams!" She sticks out one of her legs and wiggles it seductively. We all make sounds like we're impressed but, really, it just looks like a leg. A little scrawny if anything.

The two guys who were chasing each other fly out of their room again, this time the previous chaser is now the chasee and his meat cleaver is buried deep inside the back of his head.

We watch them go by, all of us horrified, except for Lithia. "Oh, don't mind those two," she says. "They're just playing."

"Maybe we should get off this floor," Jane 62 suggests. "I think I've seen enough of the lower floors for now."

"Great idea, missy," Lithia says. "Lead the way. I'm right behind ya."

"Don't you want to put something else on?" I ask.

"Nah. This is all I got anyway. What I was wearing when I did the ole…" She points a long-nailed finger to the side of her head and mimes shooting a gun.

"Suicide, huh?" Katina says. "There's a surprise."

"Suicide-murder," Lithia says with a tone of pride. "That no good bastard had it coming though, I can guarantee you that."

None of us care to ask her to elaborate, so we just smile and nod and then head back towards the elevator, Lithia bringing up the rear in her bare feet.

When we get into the elevator, though, we quickly discover that it won't go back up. All the buttons to the upper floor remain dark when we push them.

"It's because of her," Jane 62 says, pointing at Lithia. "It won't let us go back up with her in here."

"Well, don't that beat all," Lithia says mildly, dragging on her cigarette. Even though she keeps smoking, the cigarette doesn't seem to be getting any shorter.

"What should we do?" I ask no one in particular.

The elevator suddenly jerks to life, going down.

CHAPTER 11

"Uh oh," says Jane 62.

"We're fucked," Ago agrees.

Katina starts laughing yet again and everyone looks at her like she's crazy.

"You have a weird sense of humor," Ago tells her.

She makes a face at him, but then bites the inside of her cheek in an attempt to quell her giggling.

The elevator door opens, this time with a strange hissing sound and the scent that wafts inside is unmistakable.

"Oh, man," Ago says, pinching his nose closed. "Brimstone!"

Katina loses her struggle and busts out laughing. She's practically falling over, she's so hysterical.

Outside the elevator, the sounds are not nearly as identifiable as the smell. There is the sound of screaming, but it's hard to tell if it's human. Could be animal.

The hallway in front of us is even more dark and gloomy than the floor above us was. So dark that you have to squint to see anything at all.

"I'm not going out there," Ago says, punching the elevator buttons, trying to get the door to close.

Katina pushes past us, and goes out into the hallway. "This isn't real," she yells at us, grinning like a lunatic. "This can't be real! Don't you guys get it? It's like…a dream or…"

A shadow—moving fast—slams into her and explodes on impact. At the same exact instant, any meager light source out there is extinguished.

Out of all of us, Ago is the one who screams.

"What in the name of holy hell was that?" Lithia asks.

I jump out of the elevator to the place where Katina just was, expecting to have to run in either direction, either to avoid something or to search for her. Instead, I trip on something and almost fall. I manage to keep my balance but from somewhere in the gloom on the floor Katina yells, "Ouch! Watch where the fuck you're walking!"

"Sorry," I say, reaching down to where her voice came from, offering her a hand up.

"Trust me," she says. "You don't want to touch me. Oh, fuck, it smells like….it smells like shit! That thing that hit me was made of shit!"

The lights flicker, threaten to go out again, but stay on, at least for the time being.

Katina struggles to her feet and sure enough, she appears to be covered in shit. Smells like it, too.

From inside the elevator, Lithia says, "Oh yeah. I heard of those dung devils before. Never believed they really existed but I guess they do." She chuckles dryly, takes a drag off her cigarette and then starts hacking. She coughs so long and loud that Jane 62 exits the elevator with a disgusted look on her face. Not an easy accomplishment, considering she barely has features.

From behind a nearby door, someone lets out a wrenching scream that makes us all jump.

"This is where people get murdered over and over again," Jane 62 says nervously.

Ago cringes in the corner of the elevator and says, "This hotel blows. I'm glad I'm not paying to stay here."

"Oh, you're paying sweetheart," Lithia coughs. "We're all paying plenty."

As if in response to Lithia's statement, the elevator begins to shake violently, bouncing around the two of them still inside. Ago falls down and then scrambles out on all fours, his eyes rolling with fear. Lithia seems less alarmed and manages to keep her balance, stepping out into the hall with the rest of us, a sour expression on her face.

"Piece of shit," she growls at the elevator.

The moment it's empty, the box ceases its shaking and the door slides shut with a clanking thud. Ago immediately begins punching the up button and says, "Sorry, ladies, but even Purgatory is better than this."

But the elevator ignores him, refusing to open, and then it is promptly forgotten as a tremendous wind blasts us, blowing our hair and reeking of crap. We all turn as one to see the dung devil, easily as tall as me, round the corner, heading straight towards us.

A shit cyclone, splattering the walls and everything in its path with feces.

"That one is bigger," Katina shouts, turning and fleeing in the opposite direction. It doesn't take the rest of us long to follow suit, bolting down the hall with the dung devil at our heels, stinking of a Hell we never knew existed.

In the lead, Katina abruptly slams to a halt and dashes inside the nearest room, which is, thankfully, unlocked.

We all make it inside and slam the door just as the shit twister is passing on the other side.

"Hey, sorry about barging in, man," Ago says turning to face the inside of the room. "We were just—aw, fuck!"

The room we've just jumped blindly into is littered with dead babies…or, rather, pieces of dead babies. A tiny arm here, a foot over there, various heads, all in different stages of decomposition. Baby parts strewn over the floor, the bed, the desk. There are pieces nailed to the walls and ceiling, like props in some especially gruesome movie. The man standing in the center of the room is naked and holding something in his hands at crotch level, his hips pumping back and forth.

I blink rapidly, certain that I can't be seeing what I think I'm seeing, but Katina's gagging assures me that my eyes are indeed telling the truth: the guy is standing there fucking a baby's head, slamming his dick into the neck stump over and over, his eyes screwed shut and sweat pouring down his face in rivulets.

"Jesus, God," Lithia whispers and Katina starts to scream.

CHAPTER 12

The screaming is what breaks the man's trance and he opens his bloodshot eyes to look at us, and then he adds to the screaming himself. "I can't stop!" he wails as his hips keep pumping, the muscles of his ass clenching and unclenching. "I can't stop! Can't stoooop!"

I feel my stomach lurch and reach behind me to open the door. Dung devil or not, I'm getting out of this nightmare.

I manage to make it into the hallway before I puke into a slimy trail of shit that travels up the hall and around the corner. The path of the dung devil.

The others are around me a moment later and someone pats my back. I look over my shoulder to see Jane 62 watching me and shaking her head. "Humans," she says. I wait for more but then realize that is her entire statement on the subject: just "humans." Her face remains expressionless, but her tone is one of sad disgust, and I can only turn back to the task at hand and continue throwing up my guts.

"We have to get off this floor," Ago says, sounding a

little green himself. Katina is freely weeping now, Lithia supporting her with an arm around her waist.

"There has to be stairs," Jane 62 says. "In one direction or the other."

"Maybe we should split up and look for them," Ago suggests.

"No!" Katina and I shout at once. We exchange a glance and know we've both seen all the same horror movies where splitting up is never a good idea.

Ago looks vaguely annoyed but says, "Okay. But either way, we'd better get moving before another one of those shit storms comes around."

"They're the tumbleweeds of Hell," Jane 62 says quietly, almost to herself.

Lithia ignores her and says to Ago, "Before the lights go out again too."

"Right." He looks down the hall, first one way then the other and finally shrugs. "Does anyone have a preference?"

I also look in both directions before pointing to our right. "So far, the dung devils have been traveling that way. I'd rather have them at our back than run into them headfirst."

Everyone agrees that this makes sense, so we start off that way, leaving the dead baby fucker's screams behind us.

We round the corner and pass a few more doors with weird sounds emanating from behind them, but we keep moving until we see a figure approaching from the opposite direction. The distance and flickering lights make the person hard to make out at first, but it quickly becomes clear that it's a tall thin male, walking slowly, his face tipped towards the floor, apparently watching his shoes.

No one says anything at first, all of us silently dreading whatever it is that we might run into next, but the closer we get to the approaching man, the less threatening he seems until finally he looks up and, seeing us, stops.

"Don't ask me for any favors," he says, "because I'm fresh out."

Ago and I look at each other warily but continue walking with the others behind us. "Is this the way to the stairs?" I ask the guy.

He makes an irritated sound. "What the fuck did I just say? Are you fucking deaf?"

Now that we're closer, I can see he's just a skinny Goth guy, dressed in a black see-through net shirt and black pants. His hair is jet-black and spiked and he's wearing black nail polish.

We reach him and stop. "There's no need to be rude," I say. "It was just a question."

The Goth snorts at me, then looks over my shoulder at Lithia. "You got another one of those smokes I could bum?"

"No!" she snaps at him with such ferociousness that we all look at her. "Why don't you ask one of your minions?" she asks him. "Or is there no cancer in Hell?"

Puzzled we all turn back to the guy, who looks genuinely wounded. And tired. There are sagging gray bags beneath his eyes, which happen to be painted with thick lines of black eyeliner. "Fine." He waves a dismissive hand. "Fuck you too."

"Why don't you introduce yourself to everyone, Lucy?" Lithia says. "No need to be shy."

"Wait," I say, looking the skinny guy up and down. "You're Lucifer? As in…" I stop myself, remembering how he doesn't like to be called the devil. "As in, er…the dark prince?"

He makes a face at me and sighs heavily. "Not what you were expecting? My pitchfork is in the shop right now."

I frown. Who would have thought that Satan would be so snotty?

"Wow," Katina says, fully recovered from the sight of dead baby bits. "Damn, you're fucking hot!"

Lucifer looks at her and smiles slightly. I'm suddenly alarmed to see that he is actually amazingly handsome, if you can get past all the make-up and ridiculous outfit. He looks like a movie star when he smiles.

"You're pretty hot yourself," Lucifer tells Katina. "What's your name?"

"She's fifteen," I bark at him, as if he would care.

The smile slips off his face and he regards me with obvious dislike. "Who are you? Her mother?"

Pushing past him, I ask "Is this the way to the stairs? We're in a hurry."

Lucy laughs bitterly. "In a hurry, huh? To go where? To do what? Don't you morons get it? You're stuck here now. With me!"

"That's bullshit," I say. "They said we couldn't leave our own floors, too, but we did."

Ago gives me a nudge and whispers, "Knock it off, Pogue. You don't want to piss him off. He's the devil, remember?"

"I heard that!" Lucifer shouts. "Oh, screw you guys. This is what I get for trying to be nice." He squeezes by everyone and continues on his way down the hall.

"He was trying to be nice?" I wonder aloud.

Katina chases after him, asking, "So, what do you do for fun around here?"

The rest of us give each other worried looks and follow behind the two, watching as Lucy drapes an arm around Katina's shoulders. "Oh, you know," he says. "A little of this, a little of that. Want to see my room?"

"NO!" I shout, catching up and tugging at Katina's wrist. "She does not want to see your room. Come on, Katina. This guy is a loser."

"Not to mention the anti-Christ," Lithia adds from behind me.

Lucifer lets out a huge sigh, as if the weight of the world is on his shoulders. "Don't be jealous. You can come too. All of you can. Besides, we're here already."

A door opens in the wall where before there was nothing, leading into a room lit with a warm golden light.

"Fucking cool!" Katina barges forward, completely fearless, and crosses the threshold. My breath catches in my throat, waiting for whatever horrible thing is about to happen.

But nothing does.

CHAPTER 13

From the hall, we watch Katina bounce on a king-size bed, exclaiming, "It's a water-bed! Oh my God, you guys have to see this." Then she bounces off the bed and disappears from sight.

Smiling innocently, Lucy says, "See? Nothing to be afraid of. I know I have a bad reputation, but it's really quite undeserved."

"Whatever you say, pal," Lithia snorts as she enters the room in search of Katina.

"Don't go in there!" Ago calls, too late. He gives me a helpless look. "We're screwed now."

"Don't be such pussies," Lucifer says, waving us into the room after him. "I won't bite."

Ago, Jane 62 and I stand in the hall, debating with looks alone until I say, "Well, fuck it. I'm not leaving Katina in there."

I go inside and find Katina gazing out the window on the far side of the room. She glances at me and says, "Check this out."

Joining her, I look out to see the moon. Not riding

high in the night sky, as one would expect, but right below us, as though the hotel is on the moon. Dusty white craters of every imaginable size make up what should have been a lush green lawn lit with garden lamps.

"Like the view?" Lucy asks from behind us. "If not, I can change it."

"That won't be necessary," I say. "We're not staying. Come on, Katina."

By now Lithia is seated at the little dining table, tapping her cigarette into a crystal ashtray, while Jane 62 and Ago are examining framed photographs decorating one wall.

"Is this when you were little?" Ago asks, pointing to a random picture.

Lucifer peers over Ago's shoulder and grunts without interest.

Curiosity gets the best of me and I join them at the wall. Sure enough, there are photos of a young man who can only be Lucifer, at least how we know him at the moment. "Why are you standing with your arm around that big worm?" I ask, pointing.

"Ah." Lucy has wandered into the bathroom, but now comes out again, shaking pills into his hand from a brown plastic bottle. "That's me with my dad."

"Your dad?" Ago balks. "You mean…"

"Yep. The one and only." At our disgusted faces, he says, "Oh, he takes on whatever shape amuses him at any given moment. That day it was a giant worm."

We puzzle over this for a few seconds until the pills draw my attention. "What are those?"

He shakes the bottle at me. "Xanax. Want one?"

"I do!" Katina trots over, holding out her hand.

At my suspicious look, Lucifer says, "Doctor prescribed, I can assure you. Don't look so amazed. Is it so shocking that I fight a battle against depression and anxiety just like everyone else? Do you have even an inkling of what it's like to be me? Of the pressure I am constantly under?" He absently hands the bottle to Katina and then moves back next to Ago to gaze at the photos and shake his head sadly. "I used to be his favorite, you know. He used to say I was his most beautiful angel, and I was too."

"Save the pity party for someone who'll fall for it," I say. I give Katina a worried glance, watching her dry swallow a couple pills, but then I shrug it off. She's already dead. What harm could really come to her?

Which brings me to a question that has been lingering in my mind since I woke up in that river of ice. "Are we ghosts, Lucy?"

He turns away from the wall of photographs, his expression blank. "I beg your pardon?"

"We're either ghosts or zombies, right? I mean, we are dead, but at the same time, this feels exactly like being alive."

"I'm not dead," Jane 62 pipes in. "At least, I don't think I am."

"I'm dead," Lithia says. "Deader than ten day old dog shit is what I am."

"How should I know what you are?" Lucy says. "Do I look like some all-knowing, all-seeing son of fucking God to you?"

Lithia makes a clucking sound with her tongue. "Why so snippy, demon beast? Sounds like jealousy to me."

"Don't call me that! And I'm not jealous of anyone!"

"Sounds like you are."

"Well, I'm not!"

"Stop bickering," I tell both of them. "Shit, it was a simple question. Sorry I assumed you would know the answer, Lucifer."

"He doesn't know shit," Lithia says, sneering behind her cloud of smoke.

"Fuck you!" Lucy snaps. He looks furious, but not the kind of furious where you're struggling not to murder someone. The kind of furious where you're struggling not to cry.

"My," Lithia taunts. "So sensitive."

Lucifer ignores her and snatches his pill bottle out of Katina's hands. "Gimmie that. I need it more than you do."

Several seconds pass, all of us afraid to say anything. Except for Lithia, that is. She just goes right on snickering to herself.

Finally, once Lucy has taken a few more pills, he appears to calm down and gives me a serious look. "You'll probably have to ask Jay what you are."

"Jay?" I raise an eyebrow.

"You know....Jay!"

Scratching my head, I open my mouth to speak, but Katina interrupts. "Jesus!" she blurts. "Jesus fucking Christ!"

"You got it, sister," Lucy says, flopping into an arm chair, his face bored. "But I'd leave out the 'fucking' if I were you. You'll ruin his whole day if you say that to him."

"Him?" I ask, not knowing if I'm getting the concept of what they're talking about. "Who him?" Everyone looks at me like I'm retarded. "Okay, fine. I just wanted to be sure."

"Where can we find Jay?" Ago asks the devil.

Lucy waves his hand impatiently toward the ceiling. "He's where he always is, up there somewhere where else? He would never soil his reputation by coming down here to visit the damned, even though they could certainly use an uplifting word or two now and then. Much more so than those fat old farts sitting pretty in their fucking marble Jacuzzis."

"He's here?" I ask. "In the hotel?"

"Of course! You think he'd miss all this fun?" Lucy laughs dryly at the prospect.

"I want to meet Jesus!" Katina exclaims excitedly, bouncing up and down on her toes. "Can we? Please?"

I look at the others, who all shrug. "I don't see why not," I tell her.

"Sweet," Katina says. She's grinning from ear to ear until her eyes fall back to Lucifer sitting in his chair, numbing out on Xanax. "Why don't you come with us, Lucy?"

Four mouths open, screeching protest, but Lucy sits there calmly, his eyes vaguely amused. He doesn't speak until we're all finished with our objections and then he says, "Why, thank you, Katina. I think I will join you. I haven't seen Jay in quite some time, now that I think about it."

"You're just trying to spite us," Lithia growls at him.

He gives her his winning smile, his black, black eyes flashing with mischief. "That's exactly correct, old woman. Exactly correct."

CHAPTER 14

Lucifer leads our little parade out to the stairwell that we never would have found on our own, simply because it didn't exist until he wanted to climb it.

We go up several flights in silence, except for Lithia's huffing and puffing. When we arrive at a door marked 8th, Lucy swings it open and gestures us all forward. "After you," he says with a bow.

I'm a little leery—who knows where he could be leading us—but Katina marches right through like she owns the place. Like it's not the devil inviting her through, but a cute misunderstood boy. I suppose, in his own way, that's exactly what Lucy is.

With thinly veiled trepidation, the rest of us follow Katina out into the hall and I sigh with relief. The place is sparkling and clean, a lush white carpet that looks as though it has never been walked on before beneath our feet. Brass lamps with frosted glass globes sit on expensive mahogany tables, glowing bright and welcoming. From somewhere, music is playing and the song sounds vaguely familiar but I can't quite place it.

"Come along, my little piggies," Lucy says, starting down the hall. "Follow the big bad wolf."

We oblige, treading quietly, as if we're trying hard not to disturb the patrons of this five-star hotel, lest they discover our presence and have us thrown out like the bums we are.

The music swells the further along the hall we travel and then it finally comes to me: the Beach Boys, singing "Wouldn't It Be Nice."

Lucy stops directly in front of the door where the music is coming from and raps his knuckles against it loudly. He looks at us and smiles, looks at the unanswered door and frowns. He raps again, harder this time. "Open up, Jay. You have visitors."

The door across the hall opens instead and we all turn to see several nuns peeking out at us. One of them spies Lucy, makes the sign of the cross and hisses something in Latin. Another one immediately begins singing along with the Beach Boys, clapping her hands in time with the beat, completely oblivious to us.

"That's the Singing Nun," Lucy tells us. "The Flying Nun is in there too."

"You've gotta be shitting me," I say.

"Swear to God," he says dramatically.

One of the nuns pushes past the other two and joins us in the hall. The sight of her makes us grimace: blood flows down her face, streaming from her bloodshot eyes. Lucy jerks a thumb at her. "The Bleeding Nun." Then he pounds on the door with his fist. "For fuck's sake, Jay, open the fucking door!"

The door opens abruptly and a young bearded man peers out at us, followed by a cloud of smoke. I sniff and look at Ago. "Mary Jane," I say and try not to laugh.

"Jesus!" Ago says, his own nose wiggling.

"Hey, how ya doin', man?" Jesus smiles cheerily. I notice his eyes are even more bloodshot than those belonging to the Bleeding Nun.

"These kindly folks would like to have a word with you, Jay." Lucifer says patiently.

"No shit?" Jesus looks at us with his brown cow eyes. "Well, come on in!" He steps aside, taking a toke off the joint he's holding. As I pass him, I can't tell if I'm surprised by the way he's dressed, or completely unsurprised.

He's wearing worn out leather sandals (no surprise), torn dirty jeans (a bit of a surprise), and a tie-dye T-shirt with a big pot leaf on the front (a pretty big surprise). His shirt is decorated with various pins: smiley faces, more pot leaves, The Grateful Dead. His wrists are decorated with hemp bracelets and around his neck are several long necklaces, colorful beads glinting in the sunshine of his room.

"Sorry the place is so trashed, guys," he says once we're all inside. Even the Bleeding Nun has come in, trailing silently behind the nearly-silent Jane 62. Jesus starts throwing stuff around the room, clearing off the furniture for us to sit. He tosses clothes, comic books, a dirty pair of sneakers, empty soda cans, pizza boxes. All of it goes straight into a pile on the floor at the foot of the bed, which he promptly sits on, facing the TV. He takes another toke and points at the television which is playing a video game. "Mario Kart, guys," Jesus says smiling, speaking loudly to be heard over the Beach Boys. "Anyone wanna race?"

Lucifer rolls his eyes. "I told you, Jay. These people want to ask you some questions."

But Jesus isn't listening. He's started a new game, racing Mario around the track, trying to catch up to Luigi.

After a moment, he says, "Yeah, there's some cold pizza over on the…the…" He trails off, concentrating. When his little cartoon car crashes, he laughs like a child and smokes more of his joint.

Lucy clears his throat and says, "They want to know if they're ghosts or zombies, Jay." He speaks to Jesus as though the guy is a complete idiot and I'm starting to see why. I think he's toasted a few of his brains cells in the last 2,000 years or so.

"Just say no," Ago murmurs.

"Jay?" Lucy says, louder. "Can you please stop doing that for a minute?"

"I'm listening," Jay insists. "Kinda."

"Well, which is it?" Lithia demands. "Ghosts? Zombies? Spirits? None of the above?"

Jesus looks around the floor for an ashtray to stub out his roach. Once that is accomplished, he looks up at the rest of us with those earnest brown eyes and says, "That's a pretty existentialist question. I mean, who are any of us, right, man? Maybe you're not even here. Maybe I'm not even here. See what I'm saying?"

Katina has moved to the window and looks out. "Sunflowers," she says softly. "An endless field of sunflowers."

None of us are interested enough to look out with her. Instead, I look down at Jesus and say, "That's not really helping, Jay."

"Or," he continues, as though I didn't speak. "Maybe you're the whole world. The whole universe. Did you ever think of that?" He pinches his thumb and index finger together to signify something very small. "Maybe the entire solar system exists only in the pupil of your eye."

I'm beginning to feel a headache coming on and have

no idea how to respond to the son of God when he is spewing such nonsense.

"Are you sure you're Jesus?" Lithia asks suspiciously.

Jesus laughs and resumes his game.

"This whole thing is starting to get on my nerves," Ago says. "I think I liked Purgatory better."

"Fuck that," Katina replies, finally turning away from the window. "If I'm stuck here, I at least want to be stuck on one of the higher floors where we can eat something other than opera pie."

Now convinced that our question won't be answered after all, I'm inclined to agree with her. "We may as well see what we can see. Evidently, we have nothing but time anyway."

"I'm in no rush to get where I'm going, if you know what I mean," Lithia says in her cracked voice. "They can be renovating Hell till the cows come home for all I care."

"The renovations are almost finished," Lucy tells her with a smile. "I'm looking forward to it myself."

"I've been hearing that for as long as I can remember," Lithia says, clearly not intimidated.

I say, "So, I assume we still have to take the stairs, right?"

"It's not as impressive as you think up there," Lucifer says. "The lower floors are where the fun is at."

"I'm sure you would say that, but why don't you just humor us for a minute."

He sighs loudly and pouts out his lower lip. "Jay should take you. I hate it up there."

We all look at Jesus, who has just lit up another doobie and is stroking his wispy beard in a thoughtful manner. He shrugs and says, "I'm down with that."

CHAPTER 15

So, our parade has yet again increased, this time by two. Despite an endless stream of complaints, Lucifer has decided to tag along and he and Katina bring up the rear, whispering.

Ago and I follow Jesus up a flight of stairs, while Lithia, Jane 62 and the Bleeding Nun trail behind us. Jesus begins humming "Stairway to Heaven," then laughs uproariously at his own joke. The rest of us chuckle politely but I know the others, like myself, think the messiah is a major dork as well as a hopeless stoner.

Eventually, the stairs end and we all crowd onto the small landing, waiting for Jesus to open the door. He places his hand on a highly polished gold knob and say, "Okay, you guys ready?"

There are a lot of groans but I say, "Yep, we're ready."

Jesus opens the door with a flourish and then steps back. Ago and I pass over the threshold first, completely astounded. The others follow us through and I can hear soft gasps behind me. We stare in silence for what feels like an eternity.

And then, Lithia's voice: "What the hell is this? A joke?"

I blink at the vast whiteness of where we are. A bright blinding nothing. Absolute emptiness. When I turn around, I see my companions and not one other thing. We're standing on air, it seems, and the door we just passed through no longer exists.

"I told you it was boring," Lucy says.

"This is it?" Katina asks. Her voice is on the verge of breaking. "This is Heaven, where all the fucking good rich white people go? What the fuck?"

Everyone begins to talk at once, except for the Bleeding Nun, who stands silently, the blood on her face the reddest thing I've ever seen against all this white.

Suddenly I remember when I first met Salvadore and we began our trek to the Virgin City. When we first emerged from the electric forest—all that white space that crept up behind us with every step, wiping out the road, the trees, the sky. Everything.

I remember staring into that vast white space and struggling to see something—anything—and then I did. I saw some fleeting movement, too fast, too blurry to identify as anything but a trick of my imagination.

I saw something because I was trying to see something.

Looking around again, I see the faces of my companions and now they're all silent, staring at me expectantly. "What?" I say.

"What?" They all reply at exactly the same time, in one single voice.

My voice.

Stumbling back a step, I shake my head. "What's going on?"

Again, they all repeat my question, all their lips moving

simultaneously, all their voices mine.

I look hard at Katina—young Katina, so much like myself when I was her age—and watch in fascinated horror as her head begins to melt like hot wax, her features slipping right off her face and dribbling down her neck and shoulders.

All of them are melting right before my eyes, each one of them a bubbling mass of flesh colored goop, their clothes melting right along with them and puddling on the floor of nowhere.

Jesus is the last to go and as I watch, his face doesn't exactly melt, but morphs into mine. A masculine version of me, but still very clearly me.

"We were all you," the Jesus-me says. "Every facet of you that ever was."

"That can't be," I say, my voice undistinguishable from his. "No. No, no."

Jesus-me begins to melt just as the others had and I quickly turn away, concentrating on the white. I know there is something in all that nothing, something alive and moving and if I just try hard enough I'm sure to see it. If I just concentrate…

My headache worsens but I see something, a brief flittering of silver light. I screw my eyes shut and open them again, focusing hard on the spot of silver.

The single dot of silver begins to bloom, spreading out and at first I think it may be a star. But then it grows fingers, long and spidery, reaching up and up and then the whole thing resolves into what is unmistakably a tree.

A sparking electric tree.

Once I'm able to see the tree, the rest of the forest is easy to create. I think and it is: it's as simple as that.

I suppose I could have thought up anything. Maybe a city or a farm. A snowy mountain with a big lodge atop it, smoke curling up out of its stone chimney. A vast blue ocean and a warm welcoming sun.

I don't know why I created the electric forest but as soon as it's completed, I know that I made a mistake.

I know I have to try again, go back to the beginning, but I don't know how. Erasing things is not as easy as creating them, though I try hard to do exactly that, to no avail. I can't undo what I've done.

The rain is just starting to fall and there is a river of ice up ahead. I know because I put it there.

It seems important that I reach it before the black sky breaks open and electrocutes me where I stand.

And so I run.

www.ingramcontent.com/pod-product-compliance
Lightning Source LLC
LaVergne TN
LVHW050609100826
845148LV00015B/3193

9780692393147